Before You Were Born

by **Deborah Kerbel**

Illustrated by **Suzanne Del Rizzo**

pajamapress

First published in Canada and the United States in 2019

Text copyright © 2019 Deborah Kerbel
Illustration copyright © 2019 Suzanne Del Rizzo
This edition copyright © 2019 Pajama Press Inc.
This is a first edition.

10 9 8 7 6 5 4 3 2 1

www.pajamapress.ca   info@pajamapress.ca

   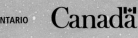

The publisher gratefully acknowledges the support of the Canada Council for the Arts and the Ontario
Arts Council for its publishing program. We acknowledge the financial support of the Government of
Canada through the Canada Book Fund (CBF) for our publishing activities.

Library and Archives Canada Cataloguing in Publication

Kerbel, Deborah, author
        Before you were born / by Deborah Kerbel ; illustrated by Suzanne
Del Rizzo.
ISBN 978-1-77278-082-6 (hardcover)
        1. Stories in rhyme. I. Del Rizzo, Suzanne, illustrator II. Title.
PS8621.E75B44 2019   jC813'.6   C2018-905916-8

Publisher Cataloging-in-Publication Data (U.S.)

Names: Kerbel, Deborah, author. | Del Rizzo, Suzanne, illustrator.
Title: Before You Were Born / by Deborah Kerbel ; illustrated by Suzanne Del Rizzo.
Description: Toronto, Ontario Canada : Pajama Press, 2019. | Summary: "Through the changing
seasons, a couple waits for their baby while the animals in the forest and ocean near their home welcome
their own young. The rhyming text describes the parents' emotions and dreams as they wait to welcome
their new baby and tells the child, as it grows how much they were loved and wanted even before they
were born"— Provided by publisher.
Identifiers: ISBN 978-1-77278-082-6 (hardcover)
Subjects: LCSH: Infants – Juvenile fiction. | Animals— Infancy – Juvenile fiction. | Parent and child
– Juvenile fiction. | BISAC: JUVENILE FICTION / Family / New Baby. | JUVENILE FICTION /
Concepts / Seasons. | JUVENILE FICTION / Nature & the Natural World / General.
Classification: LCC PZ7.K473Be |DDC [E] – dc23

Cover and book design—Rebecca Bender

Manufactured by Friesens
Printed in Canada

Pajama Press Inc.
181 Carlaw Ave. Suite 251 Toronto, Ontario Canada, M4M 2S1

Distributed in Canada by UTP Distribution
5201 Dufferin Street Toronto, Ontario Canada, M3H 5T8

Distributed in the U.S. by Ingram Publisher Services
1 Ingram Blvd. La Vergne, TN 37086, USA

Original art created with
polymer clay and acrylic wash

For Jonah and Dahlia, who wondered

—*D.K.*

To my kiddos: Ethan, Tate, Noah and Isabelle—
from tiny sparkles of hope to the wondrous
bright lights you've become, I'm so blessed
and proud to be your mom ♡♡

—*S.D.*

Before, you were...
A song in our hearts,

A star in our eyes,

A smile on our lips,
Shimmering skies,

The sun on our faces,

The full moon at night,

The tiniest murmur of tender delight.

You were…

A curve in the road, up ahead out of view,
A whispered secret that only we knew.

Sunrise ribbons ripple and flow.

Silver birches tremble below.

And now…

Slumbering sweet, awakening soon.
First bud of springtime
ready to bloom.

Asleep on our sighs,
Adrift on our dreams,

Soft as mist
floating low
over streams.

Your name in the clouds,
Your voice on the breeze,

Your kiss on a raindrop,
Your face in new leaves.

A mountain of promise,
A valley of calm,

Light of the world,
　　Curled into our palm.

Where Father Sky
meets Mother Earth,

A new family dawns
in the glow
of your birth.